GHOST BELL

Badger Publishing Limited, Oldmedow Road, Hardwick Industrial Estate, King's Lynn PE30 4JJ
Telephone: 01438 791037

www.badgerlearning.co.uk

GHOST BELL

MARK WRIGHT

Ghost Bell ISBN 978-1-78147-974-2

Text © Mark Wright 2014
Complete work © Badger Publishing Limited 2014

Publisher: Susan Ross
Senior Editor: Danny Pearson
Publishing Assistant: Claire Morgan
Copyeditor: Cheryl Lanyon
Designer: Bigtop Design Ltd

2 4 6 8 10 9 7 5 3 1

CHAPTER 1

"I wish summer could last forever," sighed Tamsin happily.

"I know what you mean," said Chase.

The two girls lay back on a grass verge, eyes closed. The sun was hot on their faces. Bees droned lazily, merging with the trickle of a nearby stream, making the two friends sleepy. This was the perfect summer holiday.

"Oi, you two! I'm bored!"

Tamsin and Chase gasped as cold water splashed over them. "Paul!" they shouted at once, sitting bolt upright.

Paul stood a few feet away in the stream, knee deep in water. He grinned slyly as he kicked up more water towards the girls. "You two are so boring!"

There were times when Tamsin could throttle her little brother. With his scruffy blonde hair and cheeky grin, he got away with murder with their parents.

"We've got all this countryside to explore and you two want to sleep?" Paul shouted, kicking up another spray of water.

Tamsin and Chase glanced at each other. They were such good friends, no words were needed.

"Right, you little git," said Chase, scrambling to her feet. "You asked for it!"

Tamsin jumped after Chase and sprinted towards her brother. Paul's eyes widened as they splashed through the stream towards him. He stumbled backwards, trying to get away, but his foot caught on a rock. Tamsin and Chase could only laugh as Paul's arms windmilled round wildly. His mouth opened in a wide 'O' of surprise, but it was too late.

He splashed down spluttering into the stream. Tamsin and Chase laughed and slapped their hands together in a high-five.

*

"That wasn't fair," complained Paul as he squelched along the path running along the edge of a field. All around were green fields and hedgerows, rising and falling ahead of them into the distance.

Tamsin and Chase followed behind, trying not to laugh. "Serves you right," said Tamsin. "Don't worry, you'll dry off before we get back to the cottage."

"You hope," added Chase. Paul looked back, glaring, then grinned and flicked water off his fingers at her.

"Let's go to the village, I've got money for ice cream," said Tamsin.

The three teenagers walked on in friendly silence, enjoying the quiet of the countryside. The summer holidays had been like this for over two weeks since they'd arrived in the village of Dewbank. Tamsin and Paul's parents had rented a cottage in the area for the whole of the summer holidays. Chase was best friends with Tamsin at school, and was chuffed to bits when her parents had invited her to spend the holidays with them.

So far it had been blazing sunshine; long days running along endless country paths; trips out with mum and dad; splashing through streams and letting the cares of the school year slip away. They hoped it would last forever.

Tamsin's promise of ice cream had lifted Paul's spirits and he was almost dry when they reached the end of the lane leading onto the village green.

Dewbank was one of those perfect little villages that people couldn't help falling in love with. There was a village green with a duckpond, a pub and a few shops, including a village store that sold the best ice cream they'd ever tasted.

Outside the shop, Paul licked greedily at a cone of mint-chocolate, while his sister and Chase talked about boys or something. He rolled his eyes and looked across the village green. Everything seemed to glow in the afternoon sunshine – apart from the bell tower.

The bell tower stood at the far end of the green. It was an ugly, dark stone needle that looked out of place in the rest of the village. It always looked to be hidden in cold shadow, even when the sun was shining. He didn't know why it was called a bell tower, he'd never heard a bell ring all the time they'd been there.

Paul licked a trickle of melting green ice cream from the cone. He couldn't take his eyes off the stone tower. There was something about it… something… he shivered, a wave of cold passing through him. His eyes scanned the height of the tower. The hands on the clock at the top were still, but… wait… was that somebody moving in the tiny slit of a window below the clock?

He shivered again, crying out as something brushed against his shoulder… "Argh!" He jumped, dropping the ice cream in shock. It splatted on the ground.

"I'm terribly sorry," said Mr Brandy. "I didn't mean to startle you."

Paul's heart hammered in his chest, but he tried to cover his fright when Tamsin and Chase walked over. "Don't worry Mr B," said Tamsin. "He's a wuss."

"I am not!" said Paul, face reddening. "The bell tower. I thought I saw somebody moving in the window."

Tamsin and Chase both laughed, but Mr Brandy whipped round to look at Paul seriously through his glasses. "The bell tower? Are you sure?"

"Don't know," mumbled Paul. He was embarrassed now.

Mr Brandy slid his hands into the pockets of his tweed trousers and smiled. "Why don't you come over to the shop and tell me about it?"

CHAPTER 2

Mr Brandy's shop had rapidly become the children's favourite place to visit in Dewbank. A light, airy bookshop, a million miles away from the usual musty, dusty village bookshops they were used to. Always at his desk in the middle of the shop was Mr Brandy, with his tweed trousers and waistcoat, almost hidden behind the widescreen, state-of-the-art computer that sat on the desk.

"Oh sorry," said Mr Brandy as Tamsin, Chase and Paul entered the shop behind him, "I'll just turn that off." He silenced the music blaring from the computer, looking slightly embarrassed. "Just listening to the new Kasabian album."

Tamsin smiled. Mr Brandy looked like a geeky English gent, but he had an air of cool about him – he even had better taste in music than any of them.

"The latest in that vampire series you like came in this morning, Chase," said Mr Brandy as Chase started scanning the shelves packed with books. He always seemed to have some new recommendation for them. "Now Paul, you seem to have had a shock."

"It's that creepy bell tower. There's summat up there," said Paul.

"I rather doubt that," replied Mr Brandy. "It's been closed up for decades. Longer, even."

"But I saw somebody," insisted Paul.

"You were seeing things," said Chase, drifting over from the shelves with a book in her hand.

"Wasn't," mumbled Paul.

"Why is the tower boarded up?" asked Tamsin.

"There lies a tale," said Mr Brandy. Tamsin thought he looked a bit uncomfortable.

"We're not going anywhere," said Chase, sitting down next to Paul.

Mr Brandy opened his mouth, looking doubtful but, seeing three expectant faces waiting for a story, he didn't have much choice.

"Oh, very well," he said, running a hand through his wavy hair and removing his glasses.

Tamsin sat on the desk and let her legs swing as Mr Brandy began. "Dewbank has a long and bloody history," he said, cleaning his glasses with the handkerchief he pulled from a pocket. "In the 1600s it was a small but thriving community of farmers, but there was something darker at its heart. Witchcraft."

Mr Brandy paused, looking at his audience – Paul peered up at him with wide eyes. He replaced his glasses and continued. "In this period of history, many were persecuted for being witches – both men and women. Anybody who had a talent for healing, for using herbs, even perhaps for delivering a farmer's pig."

Chase giggled. "A pig?"

"It's no laughing matter. Many innocents were sent to be hanged, many at the hands of Matthew Hopkins, the so-called Witchfinder General."

"He sounds great," said Paul – and meant it.

"Were all of them innocent?" asked Tamsin. "Were any of these people really witches?" Tamsin had an image of a haggard old woman in a pointy hat, cackling as she rose into the air on a broomstick.

Mr Brandy shrugged. "That's not for me to say."

"What about the bell tower?" asked
Paul impatiently.

"I'm coming to it. The local history of the area
talks of an incident in 1639. The Witchfinder
General's men had heard of a supposed witch
living in the woods who had delivered a baby for
a local woman. It was said the baby had a tail like
the devil. Nonsense, of course. Hopkins and his
men pursued this witch – she was called Aldetha
Dewbank – to the village."

"What happened?" asked Chase. Tamsin
shivered. The shop had grown suddenly cold.

"This is where the story becomes a little sinister,"
said Mr Brandy, fixing them with a piercing
stare. "The usual fate for anybody accused of
witchcraft was hanging. Aldetha fled to the
village and made her way to the top of the bell
tower, Hopkins right behind her."

He paused, then went on, "If the story is to be
believed, Aldetha and Hopkins faced each other

at the very top of the bell tower. She refused to be taken alive. Eyewitnesses said they could see fire blast from the witch's fingers into the night sky, bringing a curse down on the village. The divide between this world and the spirit world, the world of demons and witches, would be weakened forever. Before she could be taken by the Witchfinder, she jumped to her death from the top of the bell tower, bursting into flames and vanishing before her body hit the ground."

"That's brilliant!" said Paul.

"No, it's horrid," his sister replied. "A horrible story."

"History can be brutal," said Mr Brandy, shrugging. "Matthew Hopkins, the Witchfinder General, left the area never to return. It's said that if the bell ever rings in the tower, a spirit from the other side is trying to break through the divide between worlds. Of course, the bell was taken out years ago. Just in case. The clock was added years later, but that, too, doesn't work."

"Why not just knock the tower down?" asked Chase, producing some money to pay for the book she'd chosen.

Mr Brandy sat at his desk and rang the money up on the till. "I think it's fair to say that the village of Dewbank relies on a certain amount of tourist trade from the story. It's why the village was later renamed Dewbank." He handed Chase her change. "Keeping the bell tower brings people to the village. And besides," he said, his tale finished, "it's only a story."

"Still reckon I saw something up there," said Paul as they left the shop. The three friends walked slowly across the village green, glancing towards the bell tower.

"You heard Mr B," said Tamsin. "*It's just a story.*"

"Creepy one, though," said Chase.

Paul and Chase walked away across the green, heading towards the cottage and dinner with Tamsin and Paul's parents.

Tamsin hung back, looking at the ugly, black tower. It's just a story… An idea formed in her head and she smiled. "Hey, wait for me!" she shouted and ran after Paul and Chase.

As the three friends made their way across the village, they didn't see Mr Brandy peering at them from the window of his shop, a serious frown on his face.

CHAPTER 3

"I just can't stand a mystery," said Tamsin when she'd outlined her plan to the others after breakfast. They'd arranged to spend the morning in Dewbank before meeting up with their parents for lunch. Tamsin outlined her plan as they wandered along the path towards the village.

"We can't just break into a boarded-up bell tower," Chase pointed out. She'd been looking forward to a morning in the sunshine reading her new book. Now her best friend was planning to turn them into criminals.

"Why not?" asked Tamsin.

"Because it's illegal you dummy!" shouted Chase.

"Apart from that? Don't you want to find out if there is anybody up there?"

"No," said Paul, convinced his sister had lost the plot.

Tamsin stepped forwards a few paces and turned to face the others, arms folded.

"I know that look," said Paul. His sister looked at them with a determined gleam in her eyes. "Please, anything but the look."

Tamsin threw down her challenge with a raised eyebrow. "Not scared, are you?"

"Don't try it, Tam," said Chase. "It won't work."

"Wanna bet on that?" replied Tamsin with a cheeky grin. "Paul? Scared of the ghosties? Need your big sis to protect you?"

Paul glared. "I am *not* scared of ghosts."

"Well," said Tamsin, "why don't you go running back to mum and dad? They can babysit you all day. And *you* can just hide out somewhere reading your book." Tamsin turned on her heel and strode away down the path. "I'm off to find some ghosts!"

Chase and Paul looked down the path after Tamsin, then looked at each other. With a sigh, they started running after her. "Wait!"

Chase and Paul didn't see the grin of satisfaction on Tamsin's face.

*

"Still think this is a terrible idea," said Chase as they stood at the base of the bell tower, looking up. It loomed above them, dark and forbidding, as if daring them to enter.

"It'll be fine," Tamsin tried to reassure her friend, but now they were there, she wasn't so sure. It was cold, the sun never seeming to penetrate this corner of Dewbank. Over by the shops, a few people milled around, but it was still early enough for them not to be noticed.

"Coast's clear," said Paul, peering around the side of the tower to make sure nobody was coming. Since Tamsin had thrown down her challenge, he was trying to show he wasn't terrified. He had seen somebody up in the tower, he was sure of it.

The door to the tower was covered with wooden planks nailed into place. Tamsin grabbed the edge of one and pulled. It was loose and started to come away. "These must have been here for years," Tamsin said. "The nails are rusty."

With a squeal of metal on wood, the first plank came away. The three friends paused, waiting to see if anybody had heard, but the village looked as sleepy as it always did.

"This is too easy," said Chase, grabbing the next plank with Tamsin and pulling. It, too, came away easily.

Soon they had removed four planks, revealing a heavy, wooden door. It might have been the original, its surface covered with moss, some of the heavy timber having rotted away.

Tamsin reached a hand out and placed it against the door, looking at Paul and Chase. If it was locked, their adventure was going to be over pretty soon. "Shall I?" she asked.

Chase nodded and Paul swallowed nervously. "Go on then," he said.

Tamsin pushed. With a creak, the door opened.

Darkness lay beyond.

Suddenly this didn't seem like such a good idea, but Tamsin wasn't about to turn back now and lose face in front of her brother and Chase.

Without looking at either of them, she stepped forwards into the rectangle of black.

CHAPTER 4

Once through the door, dim, grey light spilled down from above onto the square entrance hall. The same black stone as outside rose up around her, but it all seemed perfectly normal. Stone steps rose up in front of her. Tamsin looked up, seeing that the steps made their way up all round the stone walls – they must take you all the way up to the bell tower itself.

"It stinks," said Paul, emerging through the door.

"He's not wrong," said Chase appearing behind him, wrinkling her nose against the smell of damp and decay in the air.

Tamsin had moved further into the hallway. "Bet we're the first ones to set foot in here in years."

"Can we go now?" asked Paul. "There's nobody here."

"We need to look everywhere," said Chase, peering up the steps. "You saw your ghost at the top of the tower, remember."

Paul's face fell. "Oh. Yeah."

"Don't know what your problem is," said Tamsin, putting a foot on the first step. "It's just a normal building. Come on, bet there's a great view of the village from the top." She started to climb, Chase close behind her, any fear she'd previously felt gone.

Paul sighed and reluctantly started up the stairs after them.

Their feet scraped on the rough, stone steps as they spiralled up and around the inside of the bell tower. They climbed higher and higher, shafts of light cutting through the murk from the narrow windows cut into the stonework.

Soon they turned one final corner on the steps. The staircase opened out as they climbed the final few feet and they found themselves stepping out into the bell tower itself.

"See," said Chase, looking around. "Nobody here."

Paul didn't look convinced. "Ghosts can hide."

Tamsin pointed upwards. "No bell." Above them, where the roof of the tower came together in a point, a wooden beam spanned from one wall to the other. Where the bell should have been lashed to the beam was an empty space. "Mr B was right."

"If the bell rings, a spirit is coming through from the other side," said Tamsin, her voice echoing now they were this high up. She looked at Paul and waved her fingers at him. "Wooooooooo…" she teased in a ghostly voice.

"Stop it," he said. "That isn't funny." He looked at his sister pleadingly. "Can we go now? I want an ice cream."

"Not yet, I want to look at the village."

Tamsin and Chase moved over to the thin window, trying not to bump heads as they both peered out. "It really is a pretty village," said Tamsin, looking down on Dewbank laid out below them. The sun glinted across the duckpond.

"It seems higher than you'd think," said Chase. "Look, there's Mr Brandy." They could see the tiny figure of the bookshop owner walking the distance from the village shop to his own premises.

"Can we go now?" said Paul in a whiny voice. "I was wrong, there's nobody here."

Tamsin began to turn. "Yeah, OK. Reckon – " she stopped suddenly. "Paul, where are you?"

"I'm here." Paul's voice seemed to echo out of nowhere.

"Stop mucking about," demanded Chase, looking around.

"I'm not! I'm right in front of you!"

The girls could hear Paul's voice loud and clear, but he was nowhere to be seen. Chase ran to the top of the steps and looked down. Still no Paul.

"Paul!" Tamsin was panicking now. "I'm warning you!"

"Tam!" Paul sounded scared. "It's getting dark. You're starting to fade away."

"If you're messing with us…" Chase said warningly.

"I'm not, I – "

Paul's echoing voice stopped suddenly, leaving Tamsin and Chase in dead silence. Tamsin shivered, her breath fogging in front of her.

"It's getting colder," said Chase, drawing her arms around herself.

The silence was shattered by a ringing bell, a deafening, clanging exploding all around them. Over and over the bell rang, again and again. Tamsin shouted over to Chase, but she could barely hear her own words over the din. Chase sank to her knees, clamping her hands over her ears.

"Paul!" Tamsin screamed, a fist of fear wrapping around her heart. Another sound joined the ringing bell, one that made her blood run cold.

Laughing.

A laugh as cold as the air in the tower, evil and harsh.

Tamsin was dizzy. She felt hands grabbing her, pushing her towards the steps. Before she knew it, Chase had shoved her out of the tower room and together they stumbled down the stairs!

"Paul's in there!" she screamed over the noise.

"We'll come back for him. Go!" They had reached the bottom of the steps and, with a shove from Chase, Tamsin found herself catapulted out through the door. She landed painfully on the grass outside, Chase right behind her.

They lay in the blissful silence, breathing heavily for a few seconds. Tamsin sat bolt upright.

"Paul!" she cried, then started as a silhouetted figure looked down on them, the sun shining in a halo behind.

"I think you two have some explaining to do," said Mr Brandy.

CHAPTER 5

Mr Brandy had listened to their story with a stony face as he strode ahead of Chase and Tamsin across the village green. Tamsin gabbled about her brother and the ringing bell – but there wasn't a bell, so how could it ring? Chase glancing back worriedly at the tower as they walked.

Mr Brandy didn't seem surprised by any of this. He walked, hands thrust deep into his pockets, face set in worry and determination.

"We have to find Paul!" pleaded Tamsin.

Mr Brandy paused in the doorway of his bookshop and placed a reassuring hand on Tamsin's shoulder. "We will. I promise."

With that, he entered the shop, Tamsin and Chase following.

"What are we going to do?" asked Chase. "Phone the police?"

"I have to tell my parents," said Tamsin.

Mr Brandy made straight for his desk and computer. "Nothing of the sort," he said briskly. "They'd only get in the way of things."

Tamsin and Chase watched in confusion. With a grim smile, the bookseller pressed a key on the keyboard. They both jumped. With a hiss of air and a hum, a section of wall slid aside, the shelves of books disappearing. Mr Brandy barely paused for them to take this in and stepped through the gap.

Tamsin nervously stepped after him, closely followed by her friend.

Beyond lay a room that was a stark contrast to the bright, airy bookshop. The chamber was illuminated by candles that hissed and sputtered in holders bolted to the dark, stone walls. Wooden bookcases heaved under the weight of ancient-looking books, and shelves were packed with odd bottles, weird gadgets and other gubbins.

Mr Brandy had removed his tweed jacket and rolled his sleeves up. He was stuffing bits and pieces from a cluttered oak desk into a scuffed leather satchel. He looked at the two friends and smiled. Was he… embarrassed?

"Ah, yes," he stammered. "I imagine you'd like an explanation."

Chase stepped forwards, saving him the bother, "Erm, Mr B, is it possible that you aren't just a friendly, neighbourhood, geeky bookseller, but some kind of demon-slash-ghost-slash-witch-hunter?"

"It seems you have me banged to rights." Mr Brandy sank down in the creaky but comfortable-looking chair at his desk. "I am a Guardian," he said, trying to explain. "A member of a secret society that, well, guards against supernatural attacks on this plane of existence." He paused for a second. "Sorry, that must sound ridiculous."

"Nah," said Tamsin helpfully. "We get it. Not as daft as some of the stuff we read in books."

"There are," continued Mr Brandy, "weak points between the dimensions. A collision of ectoplasmic energy created by magical incidents – as happened in Dewbank with Aldetha and the Witchfinder General. The story has been made more colourful over the years, but there has been a Guardian in Dewbank, watching over the bell tower, for centuries. Waiting."

"Paul's in danger, isn't he?" asked Chase.

"Yes, I'm afraid so. The gap between this world and the spirit world has weakened again."

"And my brother's fallen through the gap?" said Tamsin.

"That's about the face of it," agreed Mr Brandy. "We must retrieve him before… well, before something uses him as a means of coming through to this world."

He rose and retrieved an item from a nearby shelf. He turned and saw the worried looks on Tamsin and Chase's faces. "Don't worry," he smiled weakly, "we will get him back."

*

It was dark.

Paul didn't know how long he'd been there, sitting cross-legged in total darkness. One second he was talking to Tamsin and Chase, the next the bell tower had faded away to nothing, replaced by inky blackness and fear. There had been the deafening ringing of a bell, then nothing.

Total, dead silence.

He sensed something in the darkness. Behind him? No, in front. Or had he imagined it? A breath being taken?

"Who's there?" he said, his voice sounding small and terrified – which he was.

There it was again, like a sigh of wind.

Then somebody laughed. Harsh and mocking.

Something brushed his shoulder, freezing him with terror. Long, bony fingers, icy cold, gripping tight. Then the smell of decay caused Paul to gag and cough.

"There, there," hissed a voice in his ear. "There, there, dear boy. Soon you'll be mine…"

Paul screamed, but no sound came out of his mouth.

CHAPTER 6

The door of the bell tower creaked open. Tamsin, Chase and Mr Brandy stood in a line before it. Tamsin half expected Paul to come running out as if nothing had happened, demanding ice cream.

But he didn't.

Tamsin promised herself that, when this was over, Paul could have as much ice cream as he wanted.

"This is going to be dangerous," said Mr Brandy, peering into the rectangle of black. "I can't stress enough how dangerous, but I cannot do this alone. When we enter, keep close behind me and do exactly as I say. Do you understand?"

Tamsin swallowed nervously and nodded.
So did Chase.

Mr Brandy nodded. "Good. Time to get this over with." Without hesitating, the Guardian strode forwards into the tower, Tamsin and Chase right behind him.

"Wish I'd brought a jumper," said Chase, shivering in the cold of the entrance hallway.

"I doubt that would help," said Mr Brandy, running his hand over the stone wall. He held it up glittering with frost. Tamsin noticed the whole room was covered in a frosting of ice.

"I'm guessing that isn't good?" she asked.

"Things are further on than I'd thought," said Mr Brandy. "We must hurry."

Together they moved to the steps, Mr Brandy placing his foot on the first one. Laughter echoed around them.

"Turn back, Guardian," hissed a voice as cold as the air in the room, causing Tamsin to step back. "The boy is mine."

"I can't allow that to happen," said Mr Brandy. He seemed to have grown a foot taller, no longer the geeky bookseller. "Return him to us, and no harm shall come to you."

The cruel laugh clutched at Tamsin's heart. "I see," the voice hissed, "that you have brought me two more mortals. Their lifeforce will make the passage between worlds so… delicious."

"Give my brother back!" shouted Tamsin, causing Mr Brandy to glare warningly at her.

"So much spirit," cackled the voice. "I shall enjoy devouring you."

"Oh, whatever," shouted Chase. "Just give him back!"

"You know what we want," said Mr Brandy. "We will not leave empty handed, spirit!"

"You have been warned, Guardian. Leave now, while you are still able." With a final, hissing laugh the spirit was silent.

"The spirit isn't strong enough yet," said Mr Brandy. "Time might still be on our side…"

"What are we waiting for then?" said Chase, barging past Tamsin and Mr Brandy and running up the stairs.

"Chase, no!" warned Mr Brandy.

Tamsin moved after Chase. An icy blast of air forced her back, making it difficult to move. She saw Chase's panicked look as the blast caught her, then from nowhere an explosion of darkness seemed to surround her.

The air filled with shrieking black shapes, like rags whipping through the air. "Crows!" she heard Mr Brandy shout over the shrieking.

Everywhere Tamsin looked were sharp talons, manically flapping wings and wildly pecking beaks. The air was choked with the creatures, their shiny, black eyes glinting. "Chase!" Tamsin had lost sight of her friend in the storm of attacking birds.

Dimly, she was aware of Mr Brandy batting one of the frenzied crows away, sending it spinning against the wall with a squawk. He delved into his leather satchel, pulling out a device. It was made of twisted copper pieces, joined together around a glowing gemstone in the centre. He lifted it above his head, the stone beginning to glow. With a shriek, one of the crows dived straight for him, knocking the device from his hand.

The apparatus fell to the ground with a clang, coming to rest at Tamsin's feet. Mr Brandy was forced back against the ice-covered wall, blood pouring from a gash on his hand. "Tamsin," he gasped, "pick it up, use it!"

"Alright!" she called, retrieving the device. It felt strange in her hands, a tingle of energy passing through her arm from the metal device. Somehow, she knew what she must do.

Crying out defiantly in the storm of birds, she lifted the device above her head. The gem at its heart began to glow, the twisted strips of copper turning with a whir of gears. The gem glowed brighter and brighter, shining into the darkest corners of the room. The crows shrieked all around her, distressed at the blinding light that now blasted from the gemstone.

"That's it!" shouted Mr Brandy. "You're doing it!"

Tamsin watched through wide eyes as the crows began to thrash and buck in the air, some smashing into the wall with shrieks of terror. A low hum joined the light, growing in intensity, the whole device shaking with energy as she held it with both hands. When it seemed the light couldn't get any brighter or the hum any louder, Tamsin found herself in a bubble of silence, then:

WHOOSH!

The crows vanished in a squawk of anger, leaving the room completely silent. Chase had fallen onto the steps, arms over her head in a protective cocoon. She unfolded them and looked up, her face pale. "What happened?"

"No idea," replied Tamsin, looking in wonder – and a little fear – at the now silent device. Mr Brandy gently took it from her hands, which she realised were shaking.

"The spirit is attacking us, throwing every defence it has at us while it grows stronger." He replaced the gadget in his satchel. "This is able to absorb and repel ectoplasmic energy used to give the birds physical form."

"How?" asked Tamsin.

"Erm…" Mr Brandy opened his mouth to answer, then stopped. "Do you know, I have absolutely no idea." He grinned sheepishly, his expression changing to one of deadly seriousness as a scream from above pierced the sudden silence. It was Paul.

"Tamsin!"

Tamsin rushed forwards, taking the stone steps two at a time. Mr Brandy and Chase were right behind her.

"Hold on! We're coming!"

CHAPTER 7

Adrenalin pumping through her, Tamsin powered up the steps, her feet scraping and slipping on the sheen of ice covering them. The higher she went, the colder it got, her breath frosting in a white cloud.

Behind, Mr Brandy and Chase scrambled after her. She had to protect her little brother!

Seconds later she emerged into the bell tower itself. Ice covered the walls and floor, despite the sunlight pouring in through the narrow windows. But the room was empty.

"Paul!" she screamed as Mr Brandy and Chase joined her. They looked frantically around the chamber. "He isn't here, he isn't here!"

"He is," said Mr Brandy, urgently, "we just can't see him!"

A dull clang spread through the tower, like a bell in reverse. "What," asked Chase, "is *that*?"

"The Ghost Bell chimes, Guardian!" rasped the evil voice of the spirit.

Chase ran to one of the windows as the sunlight was snuffed out. Outside, Dewbank village was plunged into darkness. She couldn't even see the duckpond. "The sun has gone!" she said, fear widening her eyes as she looked back at Tamsin and Mr Brandy.

"Soon, all you will know is darkness." That voice again, hissing all around them, joined by the dull boom of the Ghost Bell.

"Second chime," said Mr Brandy, opening his bag. "When the Ghost Bell chimes thirteen, it's all over."

Tamsin didn't dare ask what that meant.

"Help me!" screamed a terrified voice.

The bell chimed a third time.

"Paul! Where are you?" shouted Tamsin.

"I'm here!" he replied.

"That's four," said Chase, looking up to where the bell should have been swinging from the wooden beam. "If you're going to do something, Mr B…"

"Yes, thank you, Chase," grumbled Mr Brandy, delving into his bag. "I am trying!"

"Try harder!"

"Look!" Tamsin pointed to the wall. The silhouette of a boy sitting cross-legged on the floor formed on the wall opposite them. She'd recognise that wildly sticking up hair anywhere. "It's Paul!"

"The child is payment," hissed the spirit. "Payment for my passage between the worlds!"

The bell chimed its fifth.

Behind the ghostly image of Paul appeared another shadow. A tall, thin figure of a woman, bony arms stretched out menacingly at either side of Paul.

"The gap is weakening," said Mr Brandy with sudden urgency. "Catch!" He threw a book to Chase and she caught it. "Page 42!" Tamsin quickly opened the book. "You too, Chase!" A similar book was thrown to Chase.

"The Ghost Bell chimes on!" hissed the spirit at another booming clang. "Your world will be my world!"

"Please," sobbed Paul at the seventh chime.

"Tamsin. Chase. Start reading!"

Mr Brandy stepped forwards, the twisty-turny metal device held out before him. "I will banish you, spirit!" he shouted defiantly.

"*Fira, Heo-Fan Crin-nine,*" Tamsin began reading from the top of the page. The words were meaningless to her, but their effect was instant. She could feel the room get warmer, and the spirit hissed in anger. The bell tolled once again. That made eight.

"Your time is ending, Guardian!" rasped the spirit. "Your kind grow weak!"

"While there is breath in my body!" Mr Brandy almost screamed, raising the device, which shone with blinding light.

"Noooooo!" screamed the spirit on another – the ninth – clang of the Ghost Bell. "The child will be mine!"

"*Afande Eced-ecedas Haela!*" read Tamsin and Chase together, their words mixing in and echoing back and forth around the tower. Somewhere beyond the tower, a boom of rolling thunder sounded.

With a shriek, a cloud of black crows exploded outwards, surrounding Mr Brandy. He cried out, but kept hold of the device as the birds wheeled and flapped around him. "Keep going!" he shouted.

On the tenth chime of the bell, Tamsin saw Paul's shadow on the wall solidify. She could see his face! He looked terrified, but when he saw his sister his eyes widened with joy.

"Tam, I can see you!"

"Tamsin, the gap is at its weakest," shouted Mr Brandy. "It's now or never!"

As Chase carried on reading, the light from Mr Brandy's device illuminating every corner of the room, Tamsin stepped forwards as wind whipped up from nowhere, trying to force her back. As the bell chimed again, she inched forwards, pushing against the icy gale.

"He is mine!" screamed the spirit.

"Wanna bet!" shouted Tamsin, reaching out a hand towards Paul's outstretched hand. "Take it!" she urged her brother. As the bell chimed for the twelfth time, Tamsin and Paul's fingers met and locked together.

"You've got him," said Chase.

"Now!" shouted Mr Brandy, and Tamsin pulled with all her strength, yanking back and heaving her brother's body forwards, hauling him back into the world of the living.

"Yes!" cried Chase triumphantly.

Tamsin's grin of joy changed to a scream of horror as a disembodied, bony arm lashed forwards out of the air. Thin, talon-like fingers closed around her neck as it grabbed her, trying to choke the breath from her.

"One more chime," hissed the spirit, cackling as the clawed hand squeezed tighter around Tamsin's neck. Mr Brandy, Chase and Paul seemed rooted to the spot, unable to help, frozen in a split-second of time.

A wave of rank breath passed over Tamsin. She grabbed the bony arm in both hands, trying to pull herself away from the vice-like grip.

"Let. Me. Go!" she shouted as loudly as she could, muscles straining. With a sickening, snapping crack of bones, Tamsin wrenched the arm away. The bleached white hand opened and closed frantically, trying to grab her again, then, with a crack of energy, it was pulled back to whichever dimension it had come from.

"Nooooooo!" wailed the spirit as time started again. Light exploded from the gem at the heart of Mr Brandy's device. With a crack that drove the breath from Tamsin's body, the bell tower was silent.

Nobody spoke. Sunlight streamed in shafts through the narrow windows, all traces of cold and ice gone. Somewhere, they could hear a bird singing.

Tamsin ran to Paul and wrapped him into a big hug. He let it carry on for a few seconds before saying, "Tam, I can't breathe!"

Tamsin let him go, smiling.

"How was your adventure?" Chase asked, punching him playfully on the shoulder.

Paul grinned. "I'd rather have an ice cream."

Mr Brandy coughed and all three turned. He was placing the books and device back into his satchel. He nodded at them, smiling. "Ice cream. Yes. I think I can oblige with that."

CHAPTER 8

"I think," said Paul, giving an experimental lick to the enormous cone of strawberry ice cream, "this is the best ice cream I've ever had!"

"A brush with the spirit world will do that to you," said Mr Brandy, clutching a smaller cone of chocolate chip.

Tamsin grinned as she watched the two of them. Paul was now a bit in awe of Mr Brandy as he'd been told the whole story. He'd looked around the secret room behind the bookshop with wide eyes, running from one shelf to another. Mr

Brandy had laughed as he was bombarded with questions about all the monsters he'd faced.

"Your brother's found a new bestie," said Chase with a smile.

"Yeah," laughed Tamsin. "I'm waiting for him to ask if he can be a Guardian when he grows up."

Tamsin looked across to the bell tower. Just a normal building with a dark secret. After a few seconds of silence, Tamsin said, "Thanks for helping to save Paul."

"What else was I going to do," said Chase, smiling. "If I didn't have Paul, I'd have to make fun of you instead."

Paul and Mr Brandy wandered over, their ice creams nearly finished.

Mr Brandy's face grew suddenly serious. "Now listen to me, you three. You've experienced something today that you cannot tell a living soul about. The Guardians sometimes depend on others to help in their fight against evil, and you have all shown great courage today."

"When I was little," said Tamsin, "mum and dad always used to tell me there were no such things as monsters if I had a nightmare."

"There are though, aren't there?" said Chase.

"Yes, I'm afraid so," replied Mr Brandy. "All over the world, there are weak points between the different planes of existence. Corridors for evil to travel through. The Guardians do what they can to stop that."

"If you ever need our help again, we'll be here," said Tamsin. Paul and Chase nodded.

Mr Brandy smiled. "I'm very grateful. But for now, you have the rest of your summer holiday to enjoy. The ghosts and monsters have been sent home – you three go and have fun!"

THE END